For Daisy and Rose
Riordan

First published in Great Britain in 1992 by Andersen Press Ltd., 20 Vauxhall Bridge Road, London SW1V 2SA. Published in Australia by Random Century Australia Pty., 20 Alfred Street, Milsons Point, Sydney, NSW 2061. All rights reserved. Colour separated in Switzerland by Photolitho AG, Offsetreproductionen Gossau, Zürich. Printed and bound in Italy by Grafiche AZ, Verona.

10 9 8 7 6 5 4 3 2 1

British Library Cataloguing in Publication Data available.

ISBN 0 86264 415 1

This book has been printed on acid-free paper

One Stormy Night

Ruth Brown

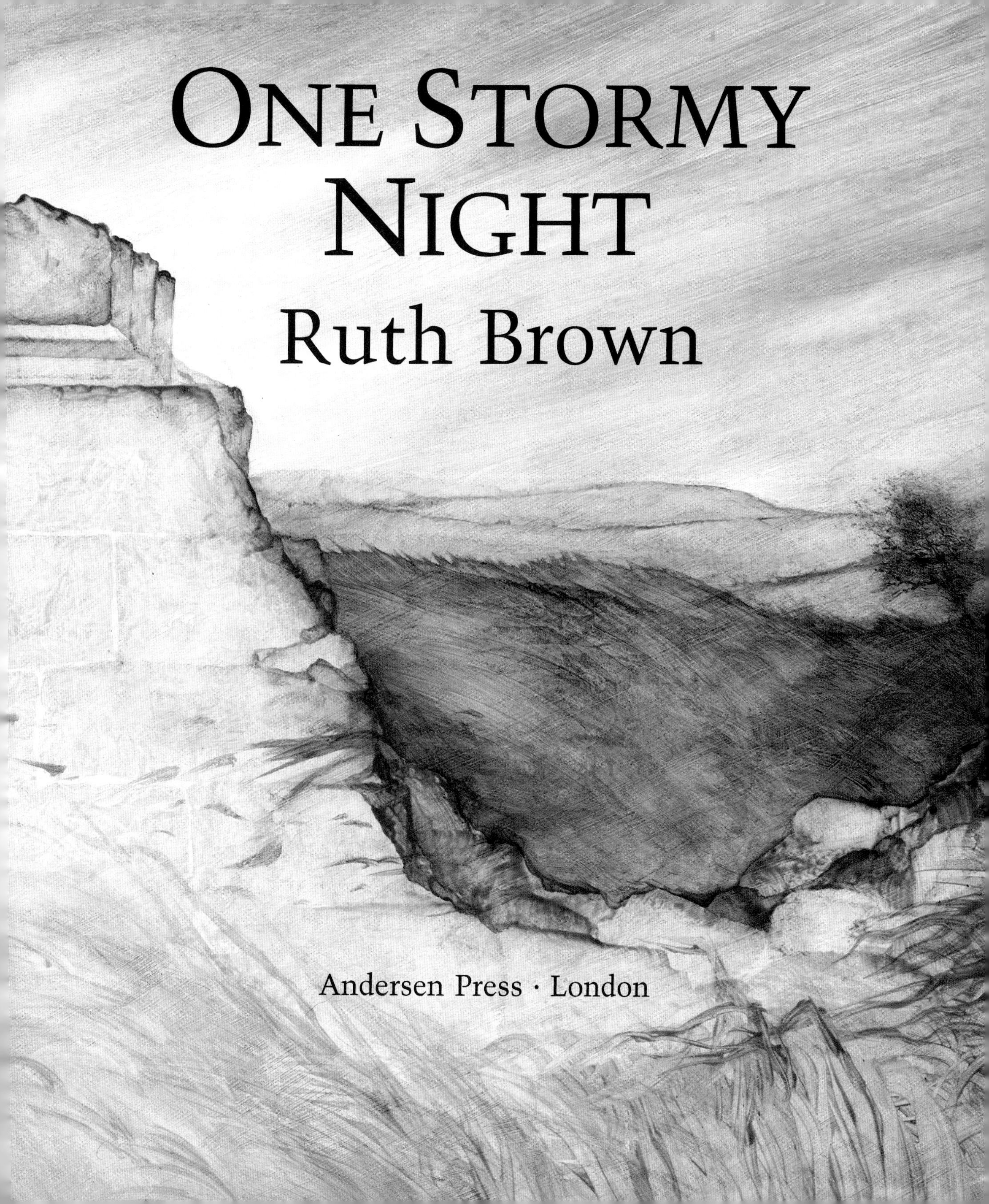

Andersen Press · London

One stormy night, the wind was howling,

the iron gate creaked,

and the black cat hissed.

Inside the house,
the fire-light flickered,

and, roused from his sleep,
the old dog barked.

The great oak door of the barn flew open.

The grey mare neighed

and a white owl screeched.

Then, just before dawn, the wind fell silent,
a bright star shone and the sky was clear.

For some a new day was beginning.

But others slept on,

in the morning sun.